To ....

For being good.

MERRY CHRISTMAS!

From Santa

D0579131

Santa is coming to London

Written by Steve Smallman
Illustrated by Robert Dunn
Designed by Sarah Allen

First published by HOMETOWN WORLD in 2011
Hometown World Ltd
7 Northumberland Buildings
Bath BA1 2JB

www.hometownworld.co.uk

ISBN 978-1-84993-198-4
Printed in China

Santa is coming to London

Written by Steve Smallman
Illustrated by Robert Dunn

HOMETOWN WORLD

"Well?"

boomed Santa. "Have all the children from **London** been good this year?"

"Well...erm...mostly," answered the little old elf, as he bustled across the busy workshop to Santa's desk.

Santa peered down at the elf from behind the tall, teetering piles of letters that the children of London had sent him.

"Mostly?" asked Santa, looking over the top of his glasses.

"Yes...but they've all been **especially** good in the last few days!" said the elf.

"Jolly good!" chuckled Santa,
"Then we'd better get their presents loaded up!"

Even though the sack of presents was

really, really big

and the elves were **really, really** small

they seemed to have no trouble loading it onto Santa's sleigh.
Though how they managed to fit such a big sack into one little sleigh
even they didn't know. But somehow they did.

"Splendid!" boomed Santa. "We're ready to go!"

"Er...not quite, Santa," said the little old elf. "One of our reindeer is missing!"

"Missing?

Which reindeer is missing?" asked Santa.

"The youngest one, Santa," said the elf. "It's his first flight tonight. I've called him and called him, but..."

Just then, a young reindeer strolled up, munching on a large carrot.

"Where have you been?"

asked Santa.

But the youngest reindeer was crunching so loudly that it was no wonder he hadn't heard the little old elf calling.

"Oh well, never mind," said Santa, giving the reindeer a little wink. He took out his Santa-nav and tapped in the postcode for London. **"This will guide us to London in no time."**

Crunch!
Crunch!
Crunch!

With a flick of the reins and a jerk of the harness, off they went, racing through the sky.

"Ho-ho-ho!"

laughed Santa.

"We'll soon have these parcels
delivered to old London town!"

Santa's sleigh flew through the starry night heading south across the North Sea. On they flew in the crisp, wintry air, crossing the coast over Hull. In the wink of an eye, the sleigh was flying above Peterborough on the right and Cambridge on the left. The youngest reindeer was very excited. He had never been away from the North Pole before.

They had just crossed Hampstead Heath
when, suddenly, they ran into a blizzard.
Snowflakes whirled around the sleigh.

They couldn't see a thing!

The youngest reindeer was getting a bit worried,
but Santa didn't seem worried.

"In two kilometres..."

said the Santa-nav in a bossy lady's voice,

"...keep left at the next star."

"But, Madam," Santa blustered, "I can't see any stars in all this snow!"
Soon they were

hopelessly lost!

Ding-dong!
Ding-dong!

Then, through the howling blizzard, the youngest reindeer heard a faint, ringing sound.

Ding-dong!

He looked over at the old reindeer with the red nose. But he had his head down.

(Red nose...that's not Rudolph is it?)

Ding-dong!
Ding-dong!

Ding-dong! Ding-dong!

There was that sound again, like church bells ringing. The youngest reindeer turned round to look at Santa. But Santa wasn't listening. He seemed to be arguing with a little box with buttons on it.

With a flick of the harness and a jerk of the reins, the youngest reindeer gave a sharp *tug* and headed off towards the sound of the bells, pulling Santa and his sleigh behind him!

"Whoa!"

cried Santa, pulling his hat straight. "What's going on?" Then, to his surprise, he heard the ringing sound.

"Well done, young reindeer!" he shouted cheerfully, "It must be Big Ben. Don't worry, children, Santa is coming!"

Then, suddenly...

CRUNCH!

The sleigh hit something as it plummeted through the snow clouds. **"You have arrived!"** said the Santa-nav unhelpfully.

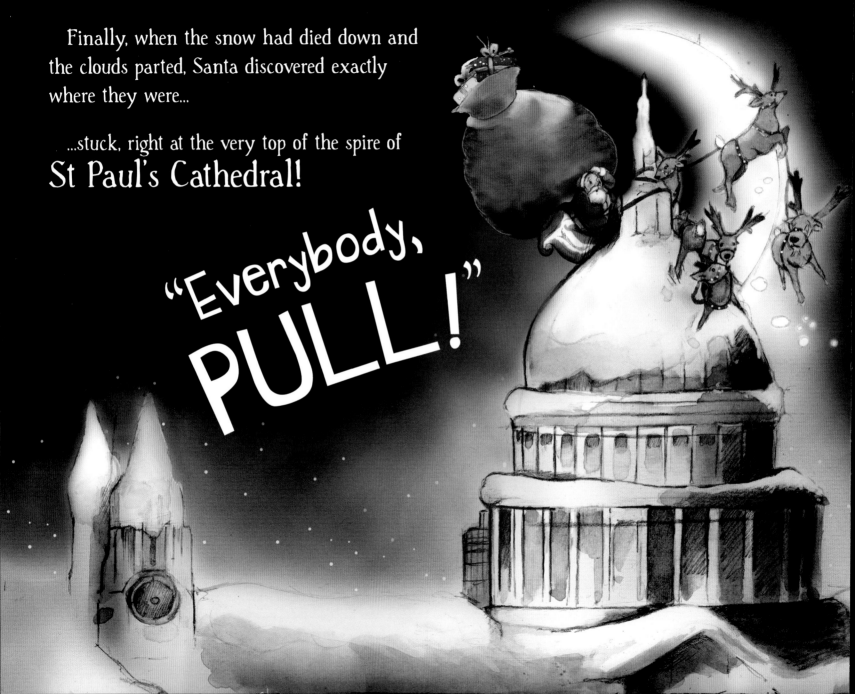

Finally, when the snow had died down and the clouds parted, Santa discovered exactly where they were...

...stuck, right at the very top of the spire of **St Paul's Cathedral!**

"Everybody, PULL!"

The reindeer *pulled* with all their might until, at last, with a
screeching noise, the sleigh scraped clear of the spire and Santa steered
them safely over Covent Garden, above Trafalgar Square, past Marble Arch
and down to Hyde Park.

Luckily, there
was no real
damage done, but
the parcels had all
been jumbled up. Santa
quickly sorted out the
presents into order again.

"Right," said Santa. "Thanks to
this young reindeer I know where
we are now. Don't worry, children,

Santa is coming!"

The youngest reindeer was
amazed at how quickly they
went. Santa never seemed to get
tired at all! And it looked like the
children in London were going
to be very lucky this year! But
the youngest reindeer was
starting to feel a bit weary
and quite hungry too!

He piled them under the Christmas trees and carefully filled up the stockings with surprises.

In house after house, Santa delved inside his sack for parcels of every shape and size.

Santa took a little bite out of each mince pie, a tiny sip of something, wiped his beard and popped the carrots into his sack.

In house after house, the good children of London had left out a large mince pie, a small glass of something and a big, crunchy carrot.

From Archway to Woolwich, from Camden to Lambeth, from Islington to Wandsworth, and ALL the places in between, Santa and his sleigh visited every house in London.

Finally, Santa had delivered the last present on his long London list.

"Great moons and stars!" sighed Santa. "It's past midnight and my sack seems as heavy as ever! I hope I haven't forgotten anyone."

Santa opened his sack to check...but it was full of juicy, crunchy carrots!

Santa shared out the carrots between all the reindeer.
"Well, done lad!" he said, patting the youngest reindeer gently on the nose.

But the youngest reindeer didn't hear him...he was too busy munching!

Then it was time to set off for home. Santa reset his Santa-nav once more
to North Pole, and soon they were speeding over the River Thames,
past Tower Bridge through the crisp, starry night.